ISBN 0 86112 791 9
© Brimax Books Ltd 1993. All rights reserved.
Published by Brimax Books Ltd, Newmarket, England 1993.
Printed in Italy.

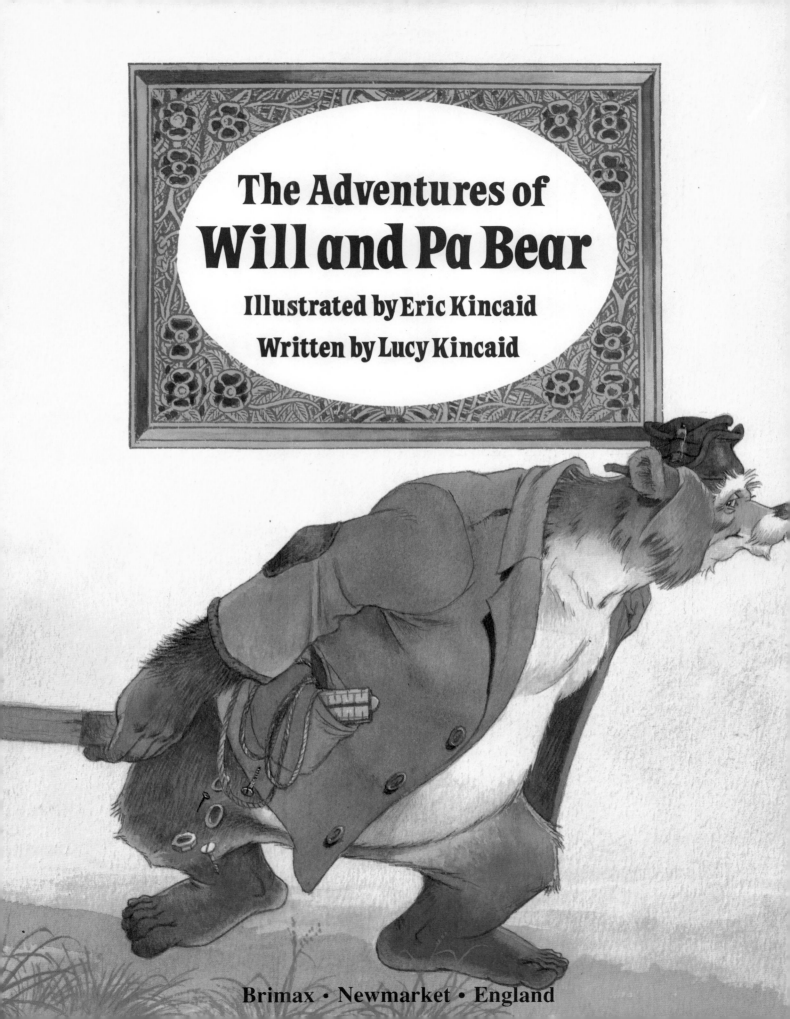

The Adventures of
Will and Pa Bear

Illustrated by Eric Kincaid
Written by Lucy Kincaid

Brimax · Newmarket · England

WILL & PA'S new friend

A Red Ear

It was early morning. Specks of sawdust were floating up into the shaft of sunlight coming through the window. Pa put down his saw and stretched his aching back.

"Have you found it?" he called, looking towards a corner where there seemed to be nothing but shadows.

There was a slither and the sound of something sliding. Something fell with a bonk.

"Oh bother," said an invisible someone.

"Have you found it?" asked Pa again, as Will, draped all about with cobwebs, emerged like a ghost from the shadows.

"Not yet," said Will. He was looking for a special piece of wood which he had been saving to make a

special bowl. He had put it somewhere safe and now he couldn't remember where that somewhere safe was. "I have looked everywhere," he sighed.

There was a shelf high under the eaves. Things were put there when they were no longer any use, but too good to throw away. Will began to feel his way along the shelf. He couldn't quite see what he was doing so he stood on his tiptoes. And up there, on his tiptoes, he saw something he wasn't expecting to see. He froze like a statue.

"Pa, come here," he whispered quietly, hardly daring to move his lips.

"What is it, Will?" asked Pa.

9

"Look there," whispered Will. He was still on tiptoe. He was still holding onto the shelf. He didn't dare let go. The only way he could point was with his nose. Pa stood on HIS tiptoes and looked over Will's shoulder. It was the only way he could see where Will's nose was pointing.

"What is it?" asked Will, trying hard not to wobble. Pa thought he could see two eyes and something fluffy.

"Perhaps it's a mouse with a beard," he said. The little eyes blinked. The something fluffy, whatever it was, brushed against Will's face. Will was so surprised he let go of the shelf and stepped backwards.

"Ow!" cried Pa, as Will stepped back onto his toes.

"That was a silly thing to do," said Pa as they both fell into a heap on the floor.

"There it goes!" cried Will.

Something small had leapt from the shelf onto the long planks in the roof and vanished.

"I'll get it down, whatever it is," said Will, already halfway up the ladder.

"Do be careful," said Pa. "It might bite."

Will came down the ladder, much faster than he had gone up it.

"Don't let it go away before I get back," he said and went up the steps to the loft. When he came back he looked like a knight in knitted armour. He was wearing an extra thick woollen jumper that reached down to his knees, a thick woollen hat pulled over his ears, a thick woollen scarf tied round his face, thick woollen socks that reached up to his knees, and thick woollen gloves.

"It won't bite me now," he said.

"It couldn't, if it tried," said Pa.

Will squeezed himself into the space between the planks and the roof. Dust started to fall. Pa waited anxiously for something to happen. Suddenly there was a shriek.

"Save me!" cried a voice Pa had never heard before. Something small, with a long tail, launched itself from the planks like a rocket and landed on Pa's shoulder.

"What have you done with Will?" demanded Pa, trying to shake the animal off. He couldn't. It was holding onto his ear as though it would never, ever, let go.

"I haven't done anything . . . there's a monster up there!"

Will's face appeared at the top of the ladder. The animal gave a frightened gasp. It buried its face in its fluffy tail and clung even tighter to Pa's ear.

"Ouch!" said Pa. He could feel his ear going red.

"It got away," said Will.

"No, it didn't. I've got it here," said Pa. "Or perhaps it would be truer to say it has got me."

Pa tried to loosen the tiny paws. He couldn't.

12

"Would you mind not holding so tightly," he said. Will started to peel off his woollen armour.

"I'm not surprised it thought you were a monster, dressed like that," said Pa. "I might have been frightened myself if I had seen you in the dark."

"What is it?" asked Will, looking at the animal closely, but not daring to touch it.

The fluffy tail stopped quivering. Will could see two little eyes peeping through it. The tail moved. Will saw whiskers and a little face with black cheeks. Whatever it was, it was just a baby.

"Who are you?" asked Will. Their noses were almost touching. "And what are you doing in our woodshed?"

"I'm Rooney Raccoon," said the animal. "And I came in out of the cold to find somewhere warm to sleep."

"A bit young to be out on your own, aren't you?" said Pa.

"My mother and father were lost in a storm. I am an orphan," said the raccoon.

"Have you any brothers and sisters?" asked Will.

"No," said the raccoon, letting go of Pa's ear.

"Have you any uncles and aunts?" asked Pa.

"No," said the raccoon climbing down to the floor. He began to walk away. His tail swept a path in the sawdust as he dragged it sadly behind him. "I'm sorry I've been so much bother," he said. "I'll go now."

Pa looked at Will and Will looked at Pa.

"He's very small," said Will.

"He's very small," agreed Pa.

"I AM very small," whispered the raccoon, walking even slower. "I am very, very small."

"You are far too small to wander about on your own," said Pa. "You need looking after. You can stay here with us."

Pa picked up the raccoon and put him on Will's shoulder.

"Ouch!" said Will as the raccoon caught hold of HIS ear. "Who would have thought such a little thing could hold on so tightly."

"Or have such a big smile," said Pa.

And that was how Rooney Raccoon came to live in the woodshed with Will and his Pa, and how Will and Pa always had at least one red ear between them.

Hatpins

Next morning Rooney was up bright and early and eager to help.

"What shall I do?" he asked, as he danced round Pa's feet. It always took Pa a long time to wake up in the morning.

"Anything," he yawned, trying not to step on Rooney, or his tail. "Anything, as long as it keeps you away from my feet."

Rooney looked at all the sawdust lying on the floor. "Shall I sweep?" he asked.

"If you really want to," said Pa. "There is a broom in the corner."

"Don't need a broom," said Rooney. "I've got a tail."

When Will came into the woodshed, just a few minutes later, he couldn't believe his eyes. There was sawdust blowing about in clouds wherever he looked. Pa was leaning against the bench with his coat on.

At least, Will thought it was his coat until he sneezed. Then the coat lifted into the air, hovered,

and settled back to fit snuggly again. It wasn't a coat at all. It was a layer of sawdust.

"What happened?" asked Will.

Pa pointed towards a small wind that was whirling round the woodshed.

"That's what happened," sighed Pa, "And I only fell asleep for a minute."

It was Rooney, chasing sawdust with his tail.

It took all morning for the dust to settle properly. It took even longer to brush the sawdust from Pa's fur, and comb it out of his whiskers and eyebrows. It had to be done properly because they were going to tea with Aunt Tilda that afternoon.

Aunt Tilda was Pa's sister and lived in the village.

"We have brought a friend to see you," said Pa, when Aunt Tilda opened the door.

Aunt Tilda looked down her long nose and inspected Rooney from the tip of his tail to the tip of his nose.

"Is he on his best behaviour?" she asked.

"Oh yes," said Pa, though he had no idea what best behaviour in a raccoon might be.

"If he is on his best behaviour he can come in," said Aunt Tilda. She set great store by best behaviour.

They hadn't been there long when there was a knock at the door.

"That will be Millie and Mollie," said Aunt Tilda.

Millie and Mollie were friends of Aunt Tilda's. They were as alike as two peas in a pod. They were as neat and as tidy as two pins in a pin box. They were never ruffled and never looked untidy.

They let Pa take their coats and their gloves, but they kept their hats firmly on their heads. They kept all their hair tucked inside their hats. They wore them absolutely straight and pinned them to their hair with long hat pins. They never seemed to take them off. Pa often wondered if they went to bed in them.

"Good afternoon," they said, each one in turn. They looked down at Rooney.

Rooney looked up at them. They seemed very tall to him. He seemed very small to them.

They folded themselves in half like two pieces of ribbon and patted Rooney's head. He went bright pink and tried to hide behind his tail.

"Oh, how sweet," said Millie. "He's shy."

"What a lovely shade of pink," said Mollie.

They couldn't resist tickling him. It was a mistake. To begin with Rooney didn't like being tickled. It made him laugh, it was true, but he didn't like it. And for another thing, it made his tail flick. He didn't mean it to happen. It just did, whether he wanted it to or not.

"Oh my," giggled Millie as Rooney's tail flicked through her dangling beads and tickled her under the chin.

"Oh my," giggled Mollie as Rooney's tail flicked the other way and did the same to her chin.

Rooney panicked. He tried to send a message to his tail but it wouldn't listen. It did what it wanted to.

The more it flicked the more tangled it got with the strings of beads. The more tangled the beads got the closer together they pulled Millie and Mollie.

Their hats collided. Their heads bumped. Their hatpins clashed and locked together like antlers.

What a pickle they were in! There they were, nose touching nose . . . bent double like bookends facing the wrong way . . . hatpins locked like antlers . . . and their beads and Rooney's tail tied together in one big knot under their chins.

They were giggling and gasping and saying "Ooh, Ooh" and trying to be on their best behaviour all at the same time. And there was Rooney, not knowing what to do for the best.

"Stop it! Stop it at once!" cried Aunt Tilda. No one knew who she was talking to. It could have been any one of them. She tried to pull them apart as though they were a bundle of straw with no feelings at all.

"Stop it, Tilda!" shouted Millie. "You will break our beads."

"Stop it, Tilda!" shouted Mollie. "You are pulling our hair."

"Stop it, Aunt Tilda!" shouted Rooney. "You are hurting my tail."

"Do something Walter," snapped Aunt Tilda, stamping her foot.

Pa wanted to laugh but he didn't dare. Will was hiding his face in the curtain trying to cover a smile that stretched from ear to ear.

"Keep absolutely still," said Pa.

"It's not easy when you are folded in half," said Mollie and Millie, from their folded up position.

"It's not easy when your tail is in a knot," said Rooney.

"Do as he says," snapped Aunt Tilda. So they did.

Carefully, very carefully indeed, Pa untangled Rooney's tail from the beads. As soon as he was free Rooney leapt into Will's outstretched arms and hid behind the curtain with him. That left Millie and Mollie still locked together by their hat pins but with their beads now dangling in long loops beneath their chins.

Carefully, very carefully, Pa drew out all the hatpins and handed them to Aunt Tilda.

Carefully, very carefully, Millie and Mollie stood up straight.

"What are you staring at?" they asked as Aunt Tilda's mouth began to twitch.

Aunt Tilda led them to the mirror.

"Oh my," said Millie and Mollie together, blushing the brightest red Rooney had ever seen. Their hats were perched on the tops of their heads like wrecked ships, and their hair usually so tidy, was in wisps round their faces. No one dared laugh because it would have offended Millie and Mollie and they had had quite enough to put up with for one day.

Aunt Tilda said she didn't think much of Rooney's best behaviour and he would have to do something to improve it. But Millie and Mollie said they quite understood about tails that had minds of their own, and it was their fault for tickling him.

The Measuring Stick

One morning Will was called to Doc West's house. He took Rooney with him. When they arrived, Doc West's sister showed them into the study.

"He's down there on the floor," she whispered as she closed the door behind them.

Doc was on his knees, grunting and groaning and grumbling. He was trying to reach something which was under the sofa. He turned round on his knees so that he was looking at Will's legs, and at Rooney's face.

"Can you get my pencil out from under there?" he said.

"If I have come all this way just to find a lost pencil I shall be cross," thought Will.

Rooney swept under the sofa with his tail. Out rolled the pencil, and three more with it. Doc put all four behind his ear and got to his feet.

"What can I do for you?" asked Doc as he brushed fluff from his knees.

"You mean, what can we do for you," said Will. "You sent for us, remember."

"So I did," said Doc. "I've got a problem I want you to fix."

He pointed to his writing table. It was covered with an untidy mess of papers and writing things.

"Every time I put a pencil down it rolls off the table and onto the floor," said Doc. "You can see how busy I am. I can't get on with my work when I have to keep chasing pencils. Sometimes I can't find them at all. I've lost five since Monday. I won't have any pencils left soon. Can you do something?"

"I'll show you what it does," said Doc. He banged his elbow on the edge of the table. The table wobbled and shook. The ink bottles rattled, papers began to slide.

Will walked round the table, twice, leaning on each side in turn as he went.

"One leg is shorter than the other three," said Will. "That is what is making it wobble. I'll make all the legs the same length."

"I'll hold the short leg for you," said Rooney.

Will couldn't see what good that would do but he knew Rooney wanted to help, so he said, "Hold it tightly then."

Rooney wrapped himself, and his tail, round the table leg as though he was a vine growing round a tree.

Doc swept all the papers into the armchair and put the ink bottles on the mantleshelf. Then Will turned the table upside down so that he could do the sawing. Before Rooney knew what was happening he was upside down too . . . AND sliding down the table leg. He didn't stop sliding until his head was touching the floor.

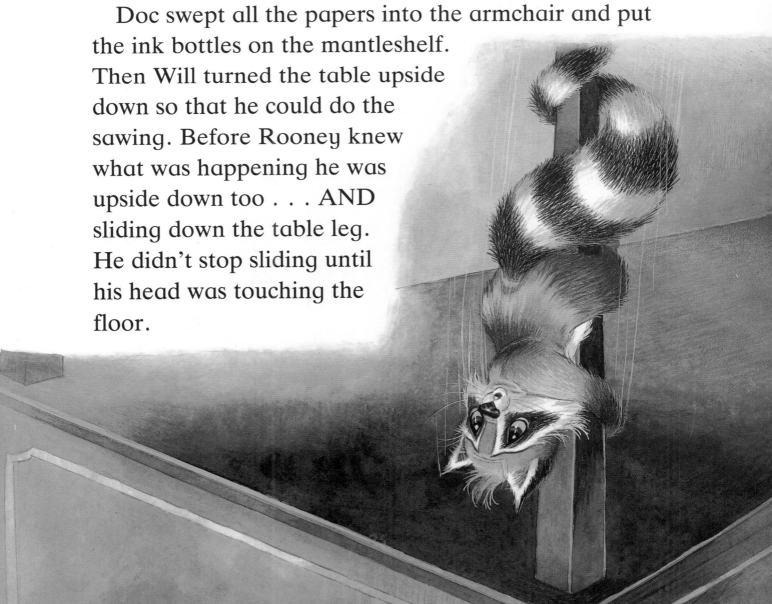

"Are you alright?" asked Doc.

"Think so," said Rooney. Everything looked so different when it was upside down.

"You can let go now," said Will. "Bring me the measuring stick please." The measuring stick wasn't in the tool bag. They had left it behind at the woodshed.

"I've got one somewhere," said Doc. "You can borrow mine if I can find it." He couldn't find it.

"I'll go back to the woodshed and get Will's," said Rooney.

"I know it's here somewhere," said Doc. He was on his knees looking under the sofa again. Rooney tried to squeeze past just as Doc began to move backwards. Doc couldn't see where he was going and

he didn't think to look. Rooney could see where he was going, but he couldn't move fast enough. If Will hadn't plucked Rooney into the air like a fish from a stream he would have been squashed.

Will was holding Rooney high in the air with his tail and his feet dangling. They were all laughing with relief at Rooney's narrow escape when Will suddenly said, "Stay just like that. Don't move anything. 'Specially don't move your tail."

"Why?" asked Rooney. "Is there something wrong with it?"

"Don't ask questions, just do it," said Will. So Rooney just did it and waited to see why he was just doing it.

Will knelt beside the table. He held Rooney so that his tail dangled beside the table leg. He moved him up, and then down again.

"I wonder what I'm doing," said Rooney to himself.

"Just as I thought," said Will. "We can use the rings on your tail as a measuring stick."

The short leg was twice as long as Rooney's tail with two more rings added on. The other legs were twice as long as Rooney's tail with three more rings added on. Will said that meant they had to measure one ring of Rooney's tail on each of the long legs and saw that much off.

Will measured. Doc made marks with his pencil. Then, while Will did the sawing Rooney and Doc went looking for other things to measure.

The sawing was finished. They were all banging their elbows on the table to test it for wobble when Pa came puffing through the door with the measuring stick.

"You left this behind," he said.

"We managed without it," laughed Will. "We have found a new way of measuring."

"Oh," said Pa. "Please explain what you mean."

They not only explained what they meant, they showed Pa what they meant.

"I never dreamed a tail could be so useful," said Pa.

Pa winked at Will. "I don't know how we will fit the new measuring stick into the tool bag," he said.

"Rooney will have to go into the tool bag with it," laughed Will.

"No, Rooney won't," laughed Rooney. "Rooney will carry it."

FOLLOW MY LEADER

Follow the Leader

"I wish they would go and play somewhere else," sighed Will. Pa and Will were working in Mrs Johnson's kitchen. They were having a difficult time. Mrs Johnson had so many children even she didn't know exactly how many she had. She counted them sometimes when they were in bed, but the answer never came out the same. The only time the house was quiet was when they were all tucked up in bed and ASLEEP. The rest of the time their little voices never stopped talking, and their little fingers were into everything.

"Who has taken my screwdriver?" asked Pa. He had put it down to look for a screw he had dropped and now it was gone.

"Not me! Not me!" shouted everyone, except the one who had it. And he was lost in the crowd.

"We will never get this job finished," sighed Pa, as Rooney rescued his screwdriver and handed it back to him.

"Can't you take them somewhere and play with them?" Will asked Rooney.

Rooney looked round at the climbing, giggling, crawling, jumping, poking, pulling, pushing, yelling, shouting, fighting, laughing crowd of children and said, "What? All of them?"

Someone else had heard Will and thought the idea a good one.

"Follow the leader . . . follow the leader . . . ," shouted the rabbit with the loudest voice.

"Must I?" asked Rooney with a pleading look at Pa.

"Please . . . ," said Pa, with an equally pleading look at Rooney. "Please Rooney, for all our sakes."

"Rooney's the leader . . . follow the leader . . . ," shouted the rabbit with the loudest voice.

"Hooray!" shouted all the other voices that only a second before had been shouting a hundred other things.

Before Rooney had time to gather his wits and escape he was being chased by a squealing, waving, jumping, skipping, running, scrambling, leaping, shouting, horde of children.

"Looks more like chase the leader to me," said Will. "Poor Rooney."

"We'll get the job done quickly with them out of the way," said Pa. "And the sooner we get it done the sooner we can rescue Rooney."

Aunt Tilda was in her garden sweeping up leaves when Rooney rushed past with his followers.

"Can't stop!" panted Rooney.

Aunt Tilda didn't know they were playing a game. She thought Rooney needed rescuing. Which he did in a way.

She ran into the middle of the mob waving her broom and shouting, "Stop . . . stop . . ."

Not one of them reached higher than her apron strings. Not one of them heard her shouting stop. They were shouting too loudly themselves.

"It's follow the leader . . . come and play . . ."
Someone caught hold of her skirt, someone caught
hold of her broom. They pulled her along with them.
But not for long. Noisy, excited children did not
frighten Aunt Tilda.

With no children getting in the way Pa and Will
soon had the job finished. They started to pack up
their tools.

"Have you noticed how quiet it is," said Will
suddenly. "I hope Rooney is alright. I hope those
children haven't chased him into the river, or locked
him in a barn somewhere."

"Of course he is alright," said Pa. "Rooney can
look after himself."

But when it stayed quiet and there was no sound or
sight of Rooney and children at all, not even in the
distance, Pa began to get worried himself.

Mrs Johnson was puzzled too. "Too much quiet isn't a good thing," she said.

They decided to investigate.

Everywhere was deserted. There were no children playing. There were no birds twittering in the hedges. There were no dogs barking in the distance. It started to seem as though there really was something to be worried about.

"Do you think the Pied Piper has passed through the village?" said Will.

"Shush," said Pa, "Don't say such things, you will worry Mrs Johnson."

They were standing in a huddle in the middle of the road trying to decide what to do when they suddenly caught the sound of Aunt Tilda's voice droning on the wind.

At least she hadn't been magicked away. "She may have seen something," said Pa. "Let's go and ask her."

"Aunt Tilda seems to have a lot to say," said Pa as they turned in at the garden gate. Her voice was droning on and on like bees in summer weather.

"She can't be talking to herself, she must have a visitor," said Will.

Aunt Tilda's voice was coming from the orchard at the back of the house.

"I don't believe my eyes," gasped Pa, as they turned the corner. Mrs Johnson just stared.

Aunt Tilda was sitting on a stool in the middle of the orchard with Rooney at her side, and all around her on the grass were the Johnson children. They were sitting with hands and feet still, and with voices silent. Aunt Tilda was telling them a story about castles and giants and magic and for the first time in their lives they were all quiet at the same time.

Rooney saw their surprised faces and put his finger to his lips.

"I didn't know Aunt Tilda could tell stories like that," said Will when the story was finished.

"More . . . more," shouted the children jumping to their feet and becoming an unruly mob.

"If you walk home quietly, and in an orderly fashion," said Aunt Tilda firmly, "I will tell you another story tomorrow."

To everyone's surprise, especially Mrs Johnson's, the children did as they were told.

"Will you teach me how to tell stories" said Mrs Johnson.

"I shall be glad to," said Aunt Tilda. "Children like to sit quietly sometimes."

"Isn't Aunt Tilda wonderful," sighed Rooney.

Tall Tales

"Is anyone at home?" asked a voice at the woodshed door.

"Come in," said Pa. "What can we do for you?"

"I want a new lock put on my sea-chest. The salt air has got into this one and made it sticky. I can't turn the key in it," said the stranger. He took a key from his pocket and showed them what he meant.

"I'll see what I can do," said Pa.

"Whatever you do, can you do it while I wait," said the sailor. "I carry everything I own in that chest and I'm off to sea tomorrow."

Pa said he would try. He knew he had a suitable lock somewhere. He found it, at last, in a box under the bench.

Rooney had never met a sailor before.

"Have you sailed all round the world?" he asked.

"A hundred times," said the sailor.

"You must have had many adventures," said Rooney.

"Thousands," said the sailor.

"You must have lots of stories to tell," said Will.

"Millions," said the sailor. "I'll tell you a few while I wait." He needed no persuading. Like all sailors he enjoyed telling stories about his adventures.

Before he began, he took off his seaboots and made himself comfortable. This was going to take a long time.

He told them stories of the South Seas and the Arctic, of being shipwrecked and becalmed, of coral islands and cannibals, of pirates and mermaids.

The stories, and the sailor's voice, went on and on and on and on. Rooney was listening as hard as Pa and Will but his ears got tired. He looked around for something to do while he gave his ears a rest.

The sailor's boots were right beside him. Rooney had never seen boots like them before. They were long and black. Very long and very black. Rooney peeped inside one. It looked like a long dark tunnel. It smelt of rubber, and the sea. It was like a magnet to Rooney's nose. He crept into it, further . . . and further . . . until he disappeared altogether and only the tip of his tail was showing.

When he reached the toe he tried to turn round so that he could come out. The boot fitted him like a sock. He couldn't turn. Neither could he wriggle out backwards. He was stuck.

The sailor was telling an exciting story about a giant sea-slug that swallowed ships when he suddenly stopped, right in the middle of a sentence.

"Go on," said Will eagerly. He wanted to hear how the sailor had escaped with his life.

"Is something wrong?" asked Pa as he saw the expression on the sailor's face change.

In answer, the sailor pointed to the floor behind them.

Something in his expression made both Pa and Will turn quickly and look for themselves. What they saw made them gasp, and without a moment's hesitation all three of them scrambled up onto the bench.

A large black slug, was wriggling and squirming its way across the floor. At least . . . they thought it was a large black slug.

"Don't let it get up here," shouted Will, trying to make himself invisible and not managing to do it at all.

"Where's Rooney?" shouted Pa in alarm, noticing for the first time that Rooney was not there with them.

"That thing's eaten him . . . look . . . I can see Rooney's tail . . . it's eaten Rooney . . . what are we going to do?" Will was jumping about on top of the bench like an indian doing a war dance. He had forgotten about making himself invisible.

"Do something!" he said to the sailor. But the sailor had only met sea-slugs in stories. He didn't know what to do with them in real life.

Rooney could tell something was happening. But he couldn't tell what. He struggled to get out of the boot so that he could find out.

"Jump on it," said the sailor. "You're bigger than me," he said to Will. "Jump on it . . . squash it . . ."

It was fortunate for Rooney that Pa had got over his fright. Pa recognised Rooney's tail. He guessed what had happened. Will bent his knees and got ready to jump. Pa caught hold of him round the waist and stopped him just in time.

"Let me go . . . ," shouted Will. "It's got Rooney. I've got to rescue Rooney."

"It is Rooney, you fool," said Pa, holding on with all his might. He was the one saving Rooney, not Will.

Will didn't look as though he believed Pa. He still wanted to jump.

"He's crawled inside the sailor's boot," explained Pa.

"Then why doesn't he come out?" said Will, shaking like a leaf at the thought of what he might have done to Rooney.

"He must be stuck," said Pa getting down from the bench to investigate.

"Are you alright in there?" he asked speaking to the toe of the boot.

"I see," he said when he heard what the boot had to say in reply.

"I was right," said Pa. "He's stuck."

While Will sat on the floor and held the toe of the boot between his knees, Pa pulled as gently as he could on Rooney's tail. Between them they managed to pull Rooney free.

"What was all that commotion about?" asked Rooney. "Did I miss something? Has something happened? And what is he doing on the bench?"

The sailor was watching and remembering so he could put everything that had happened into another story.

"You wouldn't believe us if we told you," said Pa.

"The best stories happen in real life," said the sailor as he left with his sea-chest. "Always remember that."

"What DID he mean?" asked Rooney. Will told him, and Pa was absolutely right, Rooney didn't believe a word of it.

"Now you are making up stories about things that don't really happen," said Rooney. "Mistaking a boot for a giant sea-slug . . . that's silly. No one would believe that."

And nothing they said could persuade him otherwise so they gave up trying.

Sawdust

Will had been sawing all the morning and there was a lot of sawdust under the bench.

It was still lying there when Aunt Tilda paid the woodshed a visit later in the day. Rooney saw her looking at it out of the corner of her eye and rushed for the broom.

"I meant to sweep it up this morning," he said, "But I . . . ."

"Forgot," said Aunt Tilda, finishing the sentence for him. Instead of tutting at him, as he expected, Aunt Tilda looked thoughtful.

As Rooney scooped the piled up sawdust into a box, she said, "Are you going to use that?"

"Er . . . no . . . ," said Rooney.

"Can I have it?" asked Aunt Tilda.

"I suppose so," said Rooney.

Aunt Tilda took the box from him and on the way out of the woodshed passed Will coming in.

"What are you going to do with all that sawdust, Aunt Tilda?" asked Will.

"Do I ask you what you are doing with a box of sawdust when you have one?" she asked.

"Well, no," said Will.

"Then don't expect an answer when you ask me," she said.

"She's up to something," said Will as he watched her marching away.

"She's up to something," he said again the next day, when she came to the woodshed and collected another boxful of sawdust. She still wouldn't tell them what she wanted it for. The mystery was deepening.

The next day they were waiting for her. They had the sawdust ready in a box.

As she marched away with it two shadowy figures slipped out of the woodshed and followed her. They had flat brown caps pulled down over their foreheads, and scarves wrapped round their faces.

Every time Aunt Tilda looked over her shoulder they hid behind a bush, or a wall. Once they fell flat on their faces in the grass and pretended to be part of the ground.

She didn't go home. She went to a house in the village. She was expected because the door opened as she walked up the path and she went inside.

"What do we do now?" asked Rooney, his voice muffled by his scarf.

"Look inside of course," said Will.

They sneaked into the garden and up to the window. Aunt Tilda and three of her friends were sitting round the table wrapping things in pieces of tissue paper. There were heaps of unwrapped things and heaps of wrapped things but no sign of the box of sawdust.

Rooney squashed his nose closer to the window to get a better view. It made a tiny squeak. Will squashed his nose against the window to get a better view. His nose was bigger and made a bigger squeak. Aunt Tilda heard it and looked up.

"It's a good thing we are in disguise," said Will as they quickly ducked below the level of the windowsill.

"Do you think she saw us?" asked Rooney.

"I don't think so," whispered Will. "I think we are safe."

Will was wrong. Aunt Tilda HAD seen them. She knew exactly who they were. The disguise didn't fool her.

She threw open the window and hit them both over the head with a rolled up newspaper.

"That!" she said, as she bopped Will, "is for peeping, Master Will."

"That!" she said, as she bopped Rooney, "is for peeping, Master Rooney."

And then she slammed the window shut and caught the peaks of both their caps in it.

"Oh!" said Will.

"I'm going home," said Rooney wriggling out of his cap, and he went, leaving Will to rescue the caps on his own.

The next time Aunt Tilda came into the woodshed she said nothing about what had happened and neither did they. Though she must have said something to Pa because he looked at them and laughed.

"I've got a job for you two," he said.

"Good," whispered Will, "we can escape from Aunt Tilda's steely gaze."

Will was wrong again. Aunt Tilda wanted two barrels for some mysterious purpose of her own, and Will and Rooney had to roll them all the way home for her. Aunt Tilda's steely gaze followed them every step of the way.

"There's something going on," said Will as they walked home. "I wish I knew what it was."

"I wish you would stop saying that," said Rooney. "It only gets us into trouble."

The next time they saw the barrels was at the harvest supper. Harvest supper was always held in Farmer John's barn. There was plenty of room and it didn't matter if it rained.

"Those are Aunt Tilda's barrels," said Will, nudging Rooney.

"I wonder what they are doing here?"

"I'm not going anywhere near them," said Rooney. He meant what he said when he said it.

After supper it was time to play games. Presently little parcels began to appear . . . .

"Where are they coming from?" asked Will.

"From the brantubs of course," said Pa, pointing to the barrels. "Didn't you know? Didn't Aunt Tilda tell you?"

They rushed to look. The barrels were full of sawdust, and buried in the sawdust were the little parcels wrapped in paper. The mystery was explained.

But before Rooney and Will had a chance to dip into the brantubs themselves Aunt Tilda arrived at their elbows.

"Why didn't you tell us what you were doing with

the sawdust?" asked Will.

"Would have done if you hadn't peeped," she said. "You peeped so you didn't deserve to share the secret."

She made them wait until the very last before she let them have their dip into the brantub.

"I hope there will be something left for us," said Rooney.

Aunt Tilda said they would have to wait and find out, but she knew there would be because she had counted the parcels herself.

AUNT TILDA'S
rocking chair

The Rocking Chair

The workshop door was closed and locked and Rooney was on guard at the keyhole. Pa and Will were putting the finishing touches to a special piece of work and did not want to be disturbed.

"She's coming!" said Rooney, suddenly in a panic. "What shall I do?"

"We must pretend we are not here," said Pa. "Keep very, very quiet."

They heard footsteps approaching and then someone tried the door.

"Hallo there!" called Aunt Tilda. "It's me." She rattled the door handle. "I know you're in there," she said.

Rooney had to stuff the end of his tail into his mouth to stop himself squeaking. To his relief she didn't try again.

Next time Aunt Tilda went to the woodshed, the door opened before she got there, and Rooney ran to meet her.

"Oh, I'm so pleased to see you," he said.

"Are you?" said Aunt Tilda. "Why is that?"

Rooney took hold of her arm and pulled her inside.

"There!" he said pointing to something large that was covered with a white sheet. "That's why!"

"What is it?" asked Aunt Tilda, "And why are you two grinning like Cheshire cats?" she said to Pa and Will, who were, it is true, grinning like two very happy Cheshire cats. Pa took hold of one corner of the sheet and whipped it into the air with a flourish.

"Happy Birthday, Aunt Tilda," they chorused together as though they had been practising it. Which they had.

Underneath the sheet was a chair with carved arms and a polished seat. And instead of the legs that chairs usually have it was resting on two beautiful polished rockers.

Aunt Tilda stared at it with her mouth open.

"It's for you," said Rooney, dancing round her feet with excitement.

"I've always wanted a rocking chair," sighed Aunt Tilda, patting its polished seat, stroking its carved arms and admiring its beautiful rockers.

"I've always wanted a rocking chair," she sighed

again so quietly, that only the chair heard her.

"We know you have," said Pa who had heard her the first time. "That's why we made it for you."

"We all helped," said Will. "Rooney as well."

"Try it," said Rooney, beside himself with excitement. "Try it for size."

Aunt Tilda lowered herself carefully into the chair.

"Is it comfortable?" asked Pa anxiously.

"It will do," said Aunt Tilda.

"Rock it," urged Rooney. "See how it rocks." He stood in front of Aunt Tilda and gave the chair a gentle push just to get her started. Aunt Tilda began to rock herself. Gently at first and then harder.

"It's wonderful," she said. "Just wonderful." She closed her eyes and smiled a beautiful smile that didn't go away.

She rocked harder . . . and harder. Rooney watched her smile. Her smile made him smile. He pushed harder . . . and harder.

"Steady on," said Pa, a trifle anxiously.

He should have spoken sooner, because the words were no sooner out of his mouth than Aunt Tilda began to slide. Her eyes flew open. Her hands flew to her mouth as though she was stopping a scream. She shot forward. She couldn't stop herself. Rooney tried to save her but he wasn't big enough, or strong enough, to be much good.

He couldn't stop her sliding but he did make her

landing softer. He didn't jump out of the way quick enough and as she slid from the chair to the floor she knocked him to the floor first and sat on him.

"Oh . . . oh," squealed Aunt Tilda.

Rooney tried to squeal too. He really did. But to squeal you need air inside you and Rooney had no air left inside him to squeal with.

Aunt Tilda sat on the floor going red and pink in turn. Will and Pa held their breath. They could see she wasn't hurt but they didn't know whether she was going to shout at them, or laugh, or cry, or do all three at the same time.

They managed to pull Rooney from underneath her.

Aunt Tilda looked at Rooney's flattened whiskers, his pressed down fur, his surprised face, his crinkled tail.

"Are . . . are . . . you alright . . . are you hurt?" she managed to say. The laugh that was struggling inside her didn't come out until she was sure Rooney was unhurt, then it burst out in a long merry peal.

"You make a very good cushion," she laughed. "But dear me, it looks as though someone should pump you up . . . . You really are rather flattish looking."

Rooney began to smile himself in spite of a curious feeling of being flat like a pancake.

Pa and Will picked Aunt Tilda up and dusted her down. Then Aunt Tilda set to work on Rooney and fluffed him up.

"Are you ready for another ride?" asked Will when she had finished and Rooney looked himself again.

"Of course I am," she said.

Pa held onto the back of the chair to stop it moving.

"You must promise not to rock too hard or I will take the rockers off and make it into an ordinary chair," he said.

"It won't happen again," said Aunt Tilda. "I was dreaming I was little again and swinging on my swing in the garden going higher and higher . . . ." She closed her eyes.

"She's started to dream again," said Will.

"That's quite enough of that," said Pa quickly.

Aunt Tilda opened her eyes. "You are quite right," she said. She squeezed over to one side of the chair.

"It's better if you sit in the middle," explained Rooney.

"Only when I am sitting by myself," said Aunt Tilda. "This space is for you."

"Me?"

"Yes," she said. "Come and sit beside me and we will rock together."

And that is what they did.

When it was time for her to go home, Pa and Will carried the chair and Rooney walked beside her.

"This has been one of the nicest days I've ever had," she said.

Old Sam's Cart

Pa had just bought a pile of wood and now he and Will had to find a way of getting it back to the woodshed.

"I'll lend you my cart," said Old Sam.

The cart was standing at the back of the house covered with straw and chickens.

Cluck! Cluck! The chickens didn't like being disturbed. The cart was like a giant wheelbarrow. It had an enormous wheel with an iron rim at the front, and at the back instead of wheels it had straight wooden legs, and two thick wooden handles. They had never seen anything like it before.

"Will it be strong enough?" said Will doubtfully.

"It's carried bigger loads than that," said Old Sam. "The important thing is are you strong enough to push it?"

"Of course we are," said Will.

When all the wood was piled onto the cart they could barely see over the top of it. They had to secure it with a piece of rope to stop it all sliding off again.

"Right," said Old Sam. "Off you go then . . . send my cart home when you've finished with it." He gave them a cheery wave.

As he went back into his house he gave a backward glance over his shoulder. He was smiling a secret smile, as though he knew something they didn't.

The cart was very heavy now that it was loaded and like any other wheelbarrow, whether it be small, or large like this one, the back legs had to be lifted off the ground before it could be pushed.

Will couldn't manage it on his own. Neither could Pa. They would have to take a handle each and do it between them. Somehow, that made it very difficult to push the cart in a straight line. It seemed to have a mind of its own.

If they tried to push it along the middle of the road, it veered immediately to one side and tried to go through the hedge. If they tried to push it along the side of the road it immediately crossed over to the opposite side, whether there was anything in the way or not, and more often than not there was.

Once it had got somewhere it didn't stay there. It turned about and went somewhere else. It was very contrary. And very difficult to push.

Pa and Will got very hot, and perspired a lot. They got rather tired and the tiniest bit cross. That feeling wasn't helped when passersby stopped, and nudged one another, and then went on their way grinning.

Just as they were about to give up and unload the cart and start carrying the wood home on their shoulders, they suddenly got it right.

The cart started to go along the middle of the road without the slightest wobble to the left or to the right. It went so smoothly they hardly had to push it at all.

"It has decided to behave itself," sighed Pa with relief.

"And about time too," said Will.

They came to a place where the road divided.

"Together now," said Pa, "Pull towards the right."

They both pulled hard on the handles of the cart. The cart should have turned. It didn't. It stayed exactly where it was. Pa and Will were already turning. They couldn't stop themselves turning. There was only one place to go. They collided and fell to the ground.

"What happened?" gasped Will as they picked themselves up.

"You pulled the wrong way . . . you pulled to the left," said Pa crossly.

"No I didn't," said Will.

"You must have done," said Pa. "Do it properly this time."

Again they both pulled to the right. Again the cart stayed exactly where it was. Again Will and Pa fell to the ground.

"It's got a spell on it . . . ," gasped Will.

"It's in a rut," laughed a passerby, who had been watching their predicament. "Old Sam's cart always manages to find that rut. Doesn't matter who is pushing it, it always finds that rut. Been doing it for years. Surprised you didn't know about it."

And sure enough, when they looked the wheel of the cart was in a deep rut that ran along the middle of

the road like a dried up riverbed. Wheel and rut fitted together perfectly. It was as though they had been made for one another. In a manner of speaking they had. The wheel of Sam's cart had gone that way so many times before it had worn the rut in the road itself.

"That explains why it was running so smoothly," said Pa.

"It can't stay there," said Will. "We will have to lift it out."

Pa and Will heaved, and pushed and pulled. The rut was too deep and the cart too heavy. They couldn't move it at all.

"We'll have to unload everything first," sighed Pa.

He began to untie the rope holding the wood in place.

"There is no need to do that," said one of the passersby who had stopped to watch the fun.

"And what can we do instead?" asked Will impatiently.

"Stand to one side . . . ," said the passerby mysteriously.

"What's he going to do? Wave a magic wand," said Will who was tired of the whole business and wanted to go home.

"Do as I say," said the passerby, "and you will see."

So Pa and Will, who didn't want to unload all that wood and then load it all back onto the cart again, stood to one side and hoped there really was a solution to their problem.

What happened next was almost as good as someone waving a magic wand. Passersby suddenly came from all directions, and gathered round the cart. HEAVE! HO! They all lifted together. The cart came out of the rut as easily as a pea out of a pod. And then, just to make sure it didn't fall into another rut, everyone who had helped lift it, helped push it back to the woodshed.

Rooney saw them coming and had the woodshed door open. When the wood was unloaded everyone stayed for a chat.

"It's always fun seeing what happens when Old Sam's cart is out on the road," said one of their new friends. "We always get a good laugh out of it. It only seems fair to help out afterwards." And then, as though they hadn't already done enough to help they took the empty cart back to Old Sam.

Visitors

It was a dark and windy night. Outside the trees were creaking and bending in the wind. They were casting strange moving shadows across the window. Inside the cups were rattling on the dresser. The carpets were rippling as draughts blew under the floorboards. Somewhere a door was banging.

Pa was fast asleep and snoring. Nothing would wake him until it was time to get up. Rooney had his tail curled around his ears. He was dreaming about summer days and fishing and heard nothing. Will was the only one awake. He put his head under the covers and tried to pretend he couldn't hear the door banging but he knew someone would have to get up and close it. He knew it wouldn't be Pa. He knew it wouldn't be Rooney. It would have to be him.

It was very dark downstairs. He could hear the hinges creaking on the woodshed door as it swung backwards and forwards. He was reaching out to pull it shut when he heard an unexpected sound near his feet.

Sniff . . . sniff . . . sigh . . . cough . . . sniff . . . sniff . . .

He peered down into the gloom. Holding onto the doorpost, and to one another, as though their lives depended on it, were three large bedraggled birds. Their feathers were so ruffled by the wind they looked like worn out feather dusters that were only fit to be thrown away.

Will got down onto his knees and peered into their faces.

"Why aren't you at home in bed?" he asked.

"Trees are no place for birds on a night like this," said the one nearest to the doorpost and therefore the most squashed.

It was blowing very hard. The birds were very windswept and they looked very cold. Will felt sorry for them.

"You had better come in," he said. "You can stay till the morning."

"Thank you sir, thank you sir," said the birds as they all tried to be first over the doorstep.

They wasted no time on conversation. They huddled together on the woodshed bench, tucked their heads under their wings, and went instantly to sleep.

Will went back to bed himself, amazed that anyone, especially three of anyone, could go to sleep so quickly.

"They must have been very tired," he thought.

When Will woke up next morning he thought at first the wind was still blowing there was so much rattling and banging going on. Then he noticed that everything outside was quiet and still. The wind wasn't blowing at all. The noise was coming from inside the house.

Pa woke with a start and sat bolt upright in bed.

"What is all that noise?" he asked. "And where is it coming from?"

"It's coming from downstairs," said Will, and quickly explained about the birds.

Suddenly in the middle of all the other noises they heard a frantic cry for help.

"That's Rooney's voice!" gasped Pa. He had leapt out of bed and was half way down the stairs before Will had even got his feet on the floor.

What a sight met their eyes. Rooney was racing round and round the woodshed, leaping over things, under things, through things, round things, with his tail streaming behind him like a banner. Two birds with brown wings and strong beaks were swooping after him trying to catch hold of his tail with their beaks.

There was another bird in the rafters shouting excited directions, "There he goes! He's under the bench! He's behind that plank!" And in between

shouting it was throwing things at Rooney.

"Stop! Stop this at once!" bellowed Pa. Will had never seen him look so stern.

Silence fell upon the woodshed like a thick blanket of snow. With a frightened squeak Rooney ran to Pa and leapt into his arms. "Thank goodness you have come," he sobbed.

"What is the meaning of this?" demanded Pa.

The three birds shook their shoulders and let their feathers fall sleekly into place.

"That animal . . . ," they said pointing to Rooney,

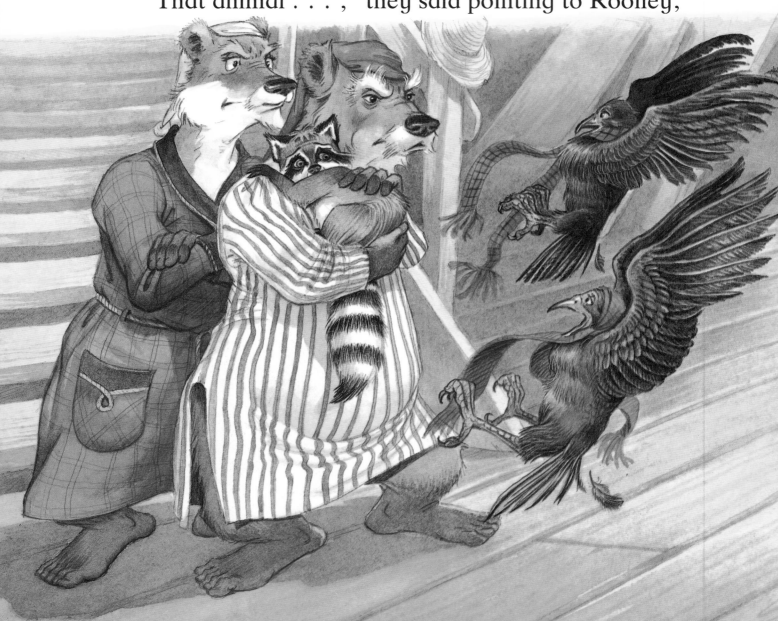

"sneaked in here when nobody was looking. We were chasing him out."

"But I live here . . . tell them I live here . . . ," sobbed Rooney into Pa's shoulder.

"He lives here," said Pa.

"He should have said," said the birds.

"Is this how you thank us for giving you shelter from the wind?" asked Will.

"But we were thanking you," said the birds. "We were chasing off an intruder."

There was no answer to that.

"It's all been a misunderstanding," said Pa, "and the least said about it the sooner it will be mended, but I would be obliged if, before you go, you tidy up the mess you have made."

The birds apologised to Rooney and said they were sorry they had chased him.

Rooney stayed well out of their way while they tidied up. He was taking no chances. Will didn't blame him.

"Next time you ask someone to stay the night make sure you make proper introductions," said Pa.

"Even if it means waking you up?" asked Will.

"Even if it means waking me up," said Pa.

"And don't forget me," said Rooney.

"I won't let him forget," said Pa.

"I wouldn't anyway," said Will.

ROONEY
to the Rescue

A Find

Will had taken his tool bag to a house in the village. A handle had come off a cupboard door and it was also loose on its hinges. Tiny Miss Smith wanted it fixed.

Rooney went along with Will to keep him company and to run errands, for Will that is, not Miss Smith.

Miss Smith had taken everything out of the cupboard to make it easier to do the job.

"This should only take a few minutes," said Will. "All it needs is a couple of new screws."

Rooney was standing inside the cupboard, holding a hinge while Will screwed it, when Miss Smith opened a downstairs window. A strong draught blew up the stairs and caught the door. It blew it shut with a bang, with Rooney on the inside, Will on the outside, and no handle on the door in between to open it.

"Let me out!" shouted Rooney banging on the door. "It's dark in here, I don't like it."

"Don't worry, have you out in a jiffy," said Will.

All he had to do was undo a few screws.

That was easier said than done with Miss Smith twittering about under his elbow and getting in the way, and with Rooney shouting and banging from inside the cupboard. He found it hard to concentrate on what he was doing. It took him rather longer than a jiffy to get the screws out.

Miss Smith was making so much noise outside the cupboard that Will failed to notice that the noise coming from inside the cupboard had stopped.

"Out you come," he said, when the door was open.

"Where's he gone?" twittered Miss Smith poking her head into the cupboard. "I didn't see him come out."

"That's because he hasn't come out," said Will.

"Then where is he?" twittered Miss Smith.

"Stop playing jokes, Rooney," said Will, looking into the cupboard himself, quite expecting to see Rooney's eyes peeping through his tail from one of the dark corners.

But he wasn't there. The cupboard was empty.

"Hallo," called a faint voice from far, far away.

"Rooney! Is that you?" called Will. But Rooney, if it was Rooney, didn't answer.

"I'd better get Pa," said Will, looking worried.

"No, no, you stay and find Rooney, I'll go for Pa," said Miss Smith and went quickly down the stairs.

While she was gone Will got the light out of the tool bag and shone it into every dark corner. He tapped round all the walls to see whether there was a secret panel that Rooney might have disappeared through. If there was one, he couldn't find it.

Presently Pa came leaping up the stairs two at a time.

"Have you found him?" he gasped.

"No," said Will. "I'm worried."

It was Pa who found the gap between the floorboards. He accidentally put his foot in it.

"That's big enough for Rooney to fall through," he said.

He got onto his knees and called through the gap.

"Rooney! Are you there? Answer me!"

"Hallo!" called Rooney's voice from far, far away.

"Help! Help!" Suddenly there was a scream and a shattering crash from somewhere downstairs.

Pa and Will found Miss Smith standing in the pantry with smashed plates and basins, and rice pudding, and boiled potatoes, and squashed tomatoes round her feet.

She was very pale. Her eyes were big and round. She was pointing to the wall in front of her. She tried to say something but she couldn't.

Will went just as pale as

90

Miss Smith when he saw what she was pointing out. His eyes went big and round, too.

There was a little grill set into the pantry wall. It was put there to let the air in and keep the pantry fresh. Looking through it were two shining eyes.

"There was no need to scream," said a plaintive voice. "It's only me."

It was Rooney.

"How did you get in there?" asked Will, putting his face so close to the grill the end of his nose poked through it.

Rooney started to explain, but Pa said, "Questions and answers later, let's get him out first."

"That is a very good idea," said Rooney.

Pa cleared everything off the pantry shelf that hadn't been knocked off by Miss Smith, then unscrewed the grill.

Seconds later a dusty, cobwebby, and excited Rooney stepped out onto the shelf.

"I think you'd better explain yourself," said Pa.

"I've had an adventure. I've found a secret staircase!" said Rooney.

"Secret staircase!" That news brought Miss Smith out of her trance. "Secret staircase? In my house? Where?"

"Behind there," said Rooney, pointing to the wall behind him.

"Knock it down . . . knock it down . . . NOW . . ." Miss Smith was VERY excited and VERY eager.

Pa and Will were just as keen to see it as she was so they set to work there and then. Soon the pantry, and everything and everyone in it, was covered with dust, and there was a hole in the wall big enough for them all to get through.

They could see a narrow, winding staircase, going upwards.

"I know the way, I'll go first," said Rooney before anyone else had a chance to get in front of him.

At the top their way was barred by wooden boards. Rooney squeezed his way through a gap between them and disappeared.

"We'll never get through there," said Will, looking over Pa's shoulder."

"We won't have to," said Pa. "It's a trapdoor."

Pa pushed with his shoulders and moved the trapdoor to one side. They went up the last few steps and found themselves standing, like sardines in a can, inside the cupboard Will had been mending earlier and from which Rooney had so mysteriously disappeared.

Miss Smith showed all her visitors the secret staircase. They were always very surprised when they went into the cupboard at the top of the stairs and came out into the pantry downstairs. It soon became the secret staircase that EVERYONE knew about.

The Glue Brush

"Oh bother," said Aunt Tilda crossly.

She had dropped her sewing box and everything had fallen out. Cotton reels had rolled across the floor. Pins had stuck into the carpet like a broken down fence. Buttons had spilled in a cascade. Aunt Tilda got to her knees and started to pick things up. She didn't like muddles of any sort. This kind of muddle she liked even less, it made her cross.

She began to fix the compartments back into her sewing box and discovered that it had broken in the fall.

"Oh no!" she cried in dismay. Her sewing box was very old. It had belonged to her grandmother. It was very important to her. She forgot all about the muddle on the floor. She gathered the pieces of her box together and without bothering to put on her coat or her hat, or even to change into her outdoor shoes, she hurried to the workshop.

"Whatever is wrong?" asked Pa. He wasn't used to seeing Aunt Tilda so close to tears.

"It's my box," she said. "It's broken . . . please . . . can you mend it for me?"

"Give it here," said Pa. "Let me look." He laid the pieces on the bench and moved them around while Aunt Tilda looked on anxiously.

"Nothing here that a bit of glue won't fix," said Pa. "Glue pot please, Rooney."

Rooney brought the glue pot and Pa put it to warm on the little stove that he kept at the back of the bench. The glue had to be melted before it would stick The way to do that was to make it warm. Pa always did that himself. He wouldn't let anyone else

touch the glue pot when it was hot.

"Glue brush, please Rooney," said Pa when the glue was neither too hot, nor too cold, but just right.

Rooney fetched it from its place on the brush rack. Pa dipped it in the glue and then while Will held two of the broken pieces for him, he carefully painted the edges with the glue. When he had finished he gave Rooney the brush to hold, took the two pieces from Will and pressed them together. It had to be done carefully and it took time.

Rooney was so intent on getting his nose under Aunt Tilda's nose so that he could see what Pa and Will were doing, he didn't watch what HE was doing with the brush. Somehow it got too close to Aunt Tilda's skirt. Will saw what had happened and secretly came to the rescue.

The glue was sticky and stretchy like treacle and pulled pieces of fluff from Aunt Tilda's skirt.

Meanwhile Pa had sorted out two more pieces of the box and was ready for the glue brush again.

"Brush," he said, talking to Rooney, but looking at what he was doing.

Rooney was worried about the sticky patch on

Aunt Tilda's skirt. He still wasn't looking at what he was doing himself.

"Ugh!" said Pa as he found himself holding a handful of sticky bristles.

"Oh . . . er sorry," said Rooney. He and Pa had a tug of war with the brush.

"Behave yourselves!" tutted Aunt Tilda. "This is no time to play games."

"I'm not playing games," said Pa.

"Neither am I," said Rooney.

Pa did the next bit of the glueing.

He hesitated before giving the brush back to Rooney.

"Be careful with it this time," he said sternly.

Aunt Tilda glared at Rooney. Rooney couldn't help seeing the sticky patch on her skirt no matter how hard he tried not to. He decided it might be safer to put the brush down before he did something else silly with it. There was still some glue in the bristles so he couldn't lay it down on top of anything. Then he had an idea. He wedged the handle of the brush between two planks of wood. It stood up like a stubby, sticky tree.

"It can't stick to anyone there," thought Rooney with relief.

"Brush," said Pa presently. "Brush please," said Pa again.

Rooney had heard him the first time and was looking about him in a panic. "It's gone," he gasped.

"What do you mean? Gone!" said Pa.

"Gone gone," said Rooney. "It's vanished!"

Will took a quick look at the back of Aunt Tilda's skirt and breathed a sigh of relief. At least it wasn't stuck there.

"It's not gone anywhere," said Aunt Tilda. "It's right behind you."

"Where?" said Rooney, twirling like a spinning top.

"Ouch!" said Aunt Tilda as something hard hit her sharply on the shins.

"Ouch!" said Will, as something equally hard hit him just as sharply on his shins.

"Stand still!" ordered Pa sternly.

As Rooney stopped twirling something hard hit him from behind. Without him noticing, his tail had touched the sticky end of the brush and now the brush was dangling from the end of his tail like a wooden leg.

"Get it off!" he shouted. "Ouch!" he shouted as Pa pulled.

His tail and the brush had been touching longer than anyone realized. The glue on the brush had had time to harden. Tail and brush were well and truly stuck together.

"Soften the glue with water," said Aunt Tilda.

Rooney sat with his tail in a bucket of water for

ages. All that happened was his tail got wet and he got stiff with sitting still for so long. The brush and his tail would not part company.

Rooney began to think of all the things he couldn't do with a brush sticking to the end of his tail.

"It will have to be cut off," said Aunt Tilda, and she reached for the scissors.

"Don't let her do it," pleaded Rooney. "Please don't let her cut my tail off."

"Silly raccoon!" said Aunt Tilda. "Catch him!" she ordered Pa as Rooney tried to run away. "Hold him still!"

Snip! Snip! went the scissors. To Rooney's surprise he felt no pain. He had been sure it would hurt when his tail was cut off, but of course his tail WASN'T cut off.

Aunt Tilda had just cut away the brush. Some of
the long hairs from the end of his tail were still
sticking to the brush and some of the hairs on his
tail were very much shorter than they had been, but
that was all. What a relief it was.

Aunt Tilda took charge of the glue brush herself
after that and then there was no more trouble with it.

"Thank you," said Aunt Tilda when the box was
finally mended.

"It took longer than I expected," . . . everyone
looked at Rooney and he looked at his toes . . . "but
thank you just the same."

As for Rooney. He vowed that the next time Pa
called for the glue brush he would find something to
keep him busy at the other end of the woodshed.

To the Rescue

"Help! Help!" Rooney came running into the woodshed, whiskers trembling and tail streaming.

Will looked up from his saw. Pa looked up from his chisel.

"What is it?" they asked.

Rooney's words came tumbling out of his mouth in a jumble.

"Rab . . . tre . . . cli . . . fall . . . riv . . . hur . . . qui . . ."

They couldn't understand a word he was saying and he didn't have time to say it all over again.

"Come with me . . . ," he said instead, and disappeared through the door in a cloud of dust.

"I think we'd better," said Pa putting down his chisel.

"I think you could be right," said Will putting down his saw.

Even with their long legs it took them a while to catch up with Rooney. His little legs were moving very fast.

"Hurry . . . do hurry . . . ," he kept saying. "Hurry . . . before something dreadful happens."

Rooney led them to the river bank. Clinging for dear life to a high branch overhanging the water was a rabbit.

Will rubbed his eyes and looked again.

"What is a rabbit doing up there?" asked Pa in astonishment.

"Someone dared him," said Rooney. "Someone said rabbits couldn't climb and he said he'd show them, and he did, but now he's stuck. You've got to get him down before he falls into the river. He can't swim. If he falls into the river he will drown."

Will didn't really see why. If he was clever enough to climb he was probably clever enough to swim. But the rabbit was tired of being clever. He just wanted to be rescued.

Will climbed up the tree. The branches were a bit thin. They had a nasty way of bouncing as he edged further along them.

"You're too heavy!" shouted Pa. "Come back before you break the branch and you both fall into the river."

Will was glad to have his feet back on firm ground. But that didn't get the rabbit out of the tree.

"Come and get me . . . ," pleaded the rabbit.

"Can't you climb back on your own?" asked Will.

"I'm frightened," said the rabbit. "I'm used to being on the ground. I don't know what to do."

"We'll have to think of something," said Pa.

Pa had an idea. He stepped down from the bank into the rushing river water. He waded across the stony bottom until he was standing directly beneath the rabbit.

He held up his arms.

"Let go . . . ," he said. "I'll catch you . . ."

"I can't!" squealed the rabbit. "I'm afraid."

"You've got too!" shouted Rooney . . . "Or you'll never get down."

But the rabbit wouldn't move.

"This is ridiculous," said Will as Pa waded back to the bank. "A rabbit shouldn't be in a tree anyway."

"Whether he should, or whether he shouldn't, he is," said Pa.

"And we've got to do something about it."

"Stand on my shoulders and we'll try to lift him down," said Pa. It sounded simple enough. Pa crouched down so that Will could step straight from the bank to his shoulders.

Carefully, oh so carefully, Pa stretched up and began to walk back into the river.

The trouble was, Pa was walking over stones that hurt his feet and made him wobble.

The trouble was, Will had nothing at all to hold onto. After one last frantic wobble when he tried to catch hold of the sky he overbalanced. Pa overbalanced with him.

SPLASH!!! Water shot into the air like a fountain. It soaked the rabbit high in the tree. It fell back onto the heads of Pa and Will as they found themselves sitting in water that came up to their chins.

They were too busy spluttering to notice what happened next. If they had they would have seen Rooney race up into the tree and along the thin bouncy branch.

Rooney had been thinking. He knew what to do now.

"Now listen to me and do exactly as I say," he said to the rabbit. "I will tell you where to put your feet, and what to hold onto."

"But I will fall," sobbed the rabbit.

"Not if I'm holding you," said Rooney. He was edging backwards, and getting closer and closer to the rabbit.

"Don't come any closer . . . you'll tickle my nose . . . you'll make me sneeze . . . and then I'll go

crashing to the ground," squealed the rabbit.

"Don't be silly," said Rooney. "I'm going to wrap my tail round you and hold you."

And if Pa and Will had been looking they would have seen the rabbit, wearing Rooney's tail round his middle like a ruff, edge slowly inch by inch along that dangerous, springy, bouncy, branch.

Twice the rabbit put his foot in the wrong place and began to slip. Each time Rooney tightened his tail round the rabbit. Each time he held on tightly himself. And each time the danger passed. At last they were both safely on the ground.

What Pa and Will did see when they had stopped spluttering was Rooney and the rabbit standing side by side on the bank laughing at them.

Pa looked first at the rabbit, then at the empty branch above his head and then back at the rabbit.

"How did you get there?" he asked.

"He probably flew," said Will. "I wouldn't put anything past that rabbit. He's probably an elephant in disguise."

The rabbit told them how Rooney had come to his rescue.

"Why didn't you do that in the first place?" asked Will.

"I didn't think of it," said Rooney, "or I would have."

"Next time there's an emergency, think before you get excited," said Pa, wiping drips of river water from his eyebrows. "Then you might save us all a lot of trouble."